CW00794439

Jacqueline Wilson

ILLUSTRATED BY NICK SHARRATT

Hetty Feather
Journal

DOUBLEDAY

CHECK OUT JACQUELINE WILSON'S OFFICIAL WEBSITE!

There's a whole Jacqueline Wilson town to explore! You can generate your own special username, customise your online bedroom, test your knowledge of Jacqueline's books with fun quizzes and puzzles, and upload book reviews. There's lots of fun stuff to discover, including competitions, book trailers, and Jacqueline's scrapbook. And if you love writing, visit the special storytelling area!

Plus, you can hear the latest news from Jacqueline in her monthly diary, find out whether she's doing events near you, read her fan-mail replies, and chat to other fans on the message boards!

www.jacquelinewilson.co.uk

THIS JOURNAL
BELONGS TO:

Name: Violet   Thurtle

_____

Address: _____

_____

_____

Phone number: _____

Email: _____

Birthday: 1st october

EVERYTHING YOU NEED TO KNOW ABOUT . . . HETTY FEATHER!

★ Hetty was born almost 150 years ago, in 1876 – so she is a Victorian.

★ Hetty has fiery red hair and bright blue eyes.

★ Her best friend in the country is her foster-brother, Jem. At the Foundling Hospital, her best friend is Polly.

★ Hetty's other close friends include Fantastic Freda, the Female Giant; Madame Adeline and Diamond; and kind, thoughtful Janet.

★ Hetty's enemies at the Hospital are Matron Pigface, Matron Stinking Bottomly, and horrid Sheila!

★ Hetty's Foundling Number is 25629.

★ Hetty discovers that her real name is Sapphire Battersea.

★ She also creates a third name for herself when she becomes a performer on the stage: Emerald Star!

★ Hetty desperately wants to be a writer, and takes pride in writing her memoirs. Hetty meets two real writers herself: Miss Sarah Smith, and Mr Charles Buchanan.

★ When she's very young, Hetty believes she will grow up and marry Jem – but she also meets a new sweetheart when she is working as a maid: Bertie.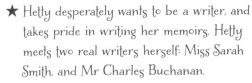

★ Hetty spends her first years in the countryside, and then lives in London – but discovers that her parents were originally from a fishing village in Yorkshire.

★ Hetty grows up with foster-siblings, but is amazed to discover that she has a half-brother and half-sister!

★ Hetty falls in love with the circus when she is very small – she's particularly enraptured with the glamorous Madame Adeline.

THE VICTORIANS!

★ Queen Victoria ruled for sixty-three years. She was only 18 years old when she became Queen!

★ Queen Victoria married Prince Albert, and they had nine children together. Queen Victoria's descendants are still on the British throne today – Queen Elizabeth II is Queen Victoria's great-great-granddaughter!

★ The Victorians were famous for being very straight-laced and reserved – although Hetty Feather couldn't be described as either of those things!

★ Victorian families were often very large. It wasn't unusual for a Victorian couple to have as many as ten children. Imagine having nine brothers and sisters!

★ Many Victorians lived in extreme poverty. Children from very poor families wouldn't have gone to school; instead, they'd go to work in factories, mines, or as chimney sweeps or shoe blacks; or they might have sold items like matches or flowers on the streets (like Hetty's friend Sissy). In fact, lots of people were so poor that they were forced into workhouses, where they worked in terrible conditions in exchange for scraps of food and a place to sleep.

Sissy

★ Some Victorians, though, were extremely rich! Boys from wealthy families were sent to school and often to university. Wealthy girls, on the other hand, might have been sent to a 'finishing school' where they would learn to become a 'lady', taking lessons in things like French, singing and dancing, playing the piano, and even curtseying.

★ Rich Victorian women were not expected to work; instead they would be in charge of their household, and manage a team of servants. Wealthy Victorian couples would often employ a nanny to take care of their children for them.

★ Some of the most important inventions came about during the Victoria era, including cars, photography, electric light bulbs, sewing machines, post boxes and the first ever postage stamp – called the Penny Black.

★ The London Underground opened during the Victorian times, known as the tube. Jelly babies and chocolate Easter eggs were Victorian creations, too!

★ Some of the most important books ever written were by Victorian authors. You can find out a bit more about them later on!

FAMOUS VICTORIANS!

How many of these famous Victorians have you heard of?

★ Elizabeth Fry: a prisoner reformer. Elizabeth was horrified by the terrible conditions of Victorian prisons, and worked hard to improve them. She also set up a nightly shelter for the homeless. She appears on the English £5 note!

★ Alexander Graham Bell: the inventor of the telephone.

★ Joseph Lister: a Scottish doctor who realized how important it was to keep medical equipment clean and germ-free during operations.

★ David Livingstone: a very famous explorer, who trekked through Africa.

★ Sir Titus Salt: a businessman who built an entire village, including a library, a hospital and a concert hall, for all his workers to live in. The village was eventually named after him – Saltaire – and lots of the streets were named after his family.

WHICH VICTORIAN WOULD YOU BE?

Find a coin and flip it!

If you get heads, you're Princess Beatrice, Queen Victoria's youngest daughter.

If you get tails, you're Mary March, a poor flower-seller living on the streets of London.

Whichever character you are, try to imagine what life might have been like for you. You could even write a story about your character.

Here are some words to inspire you:
Wealthy ★ Poverty ★ Starving ★ Royalty ★ Luxury
Buckingham Palace ★ London ★ Slums ★ Workhouse
Sisters ★ Orphan ★ Gruel ★ Cold ★ Mother ★ Parties
Nannies ★ Jubilee ★ Tired ★ Flowers ★ Rags ★ Ballgown

HETTY FEATHER QUIZ!

How well do you know the world of Hetty Feather?
Take this quiz to find out!

1. Hetty's Foundling Number is 25629. What is her foster-brother Gideon's number?

2. Name Hetty's foster-mother, who looks after Hetty when she lives in the country.

3. One of Hetty's favourite acts at Tanglefield's Travelling Circus is named Elijah. What sort of creature is he?

4. Hetty meets a girl named Sissy when she runs away from the rest of the foundlings at Queen Victoria's Golden Jubilee. What does Sissy sell to make money?

5. What position is Hetty given when she leaves the Foundling Hospital and goes to work for Mr Charles Buchanan?

6. At the same time, Gideon is sent out from the Hospital to do what?

7. Hetty attends a séance led by a lady named Madame Berenice. Who does Hetty's fellow servant, Sarah, hope to speak to at the séance?

8. What mythical creature does Hetty dress up as when she joins Mr Clarendon's Seaside Curiosities?

9. What are the names of Hetty's half-sister and half-brother?

10. Jem gives Hetty a silver sixpence necklace for Christmas. What does Hetty give to Jem?

11. Hetty very naughtily sneaks a peek at a friend's private diary. Whose?

12. When Hetty joins Tanglefield's Travelling Circus, what job does she persuade Mr Tanglefield to give her?

13. Hetty befriends the little acrobat, Diamond, when she joins the circus. What is the name of the troupe of acrobats that Diamond performs with?

14. Hetty is amazed to meet her old friend Polly at one of her circus performances – but Polly's new family have given her a new name. What is it?

15. Hetty helps to rescue Mavis, another of the circus acts, when she gets stuck up a tree during a storm. What is Mavis?

WRITE YOUR OWN LIFE STORY . . . LIKE HETTY!

Hetty starts writing her memoirs after meeting Miss Sarah Smith, who buys her a beautiful scarlet, orange and gold notebook. She begins with the day she was born – even though she can't really remember that far back!

Why don't you try writing your life story so far? If you need ideas, you could ask your parents, grandparents or older siblings for help, as they might tell you some interesting or funny stories about you when you were very little.

You could write a new chapter for each year of your life – or, if you have lived in different places or attended different schools, you could split your story into new parts for each different time in your life so far.

Start here, and if you find you've got lots and lots to say, see if you can find a pretty notebook to continue in, just like Hetty!

_____

_____

_____

PUZZLE PAGE!

One of the most important parts of Hetty's story takes place at Tanglefield's Travelling Circus. Can you find these circus words in the wordsearch below? You could set yourself a challenge of five minutes to find them all!

Adeline ★ Big Top ★ Circus ★ Clown ★ Diamond
Lion ★ Marvel ★ Monkey ★ Star ★ Tightrope ★ Wagon

P	O	T	G	I	B	Z	Y	W	O	L
R	M	C	M	Q	Y	H	F	A	P	Q
K	A	L	A	F	A	Z	L	G	H	W
Y	C	I	R	C	U	S	J	O	K	S
E	L	O	D	Q	G	E	K	N	R	D
K	O	N	P	J	A	C	D	E	J	A
N	W	K	L	J	D	I	F	T	I	F
O	N	K	N	T	E	L	G	F	E	B
M	A	R	V	E	L	O	H	R	P	V
A	T	A	S	D	I	N	E	E	O	E
H	S	T	A	Z	N	B	A	K	R	W
A	O	S	M	X	E	O	B	J	T	Y
D	L	G	T	N	I	P	M	H	H	H
H	N	X	M	O	C	B	V	A	G	S
T	N	U	A	G	T	Y	B	A	I	F
H	B	O	I	Q	S	V	M	F	T	D

Who said it? Can you match the lines below
to the characters who said them?

Matron Bottomly ★ Madame Adeline ★ Ida ★ Eliza
Gideon ★ Sissy ★ Miss Sarah Smith

1. Now, Hetty, it's your turn to sing for your supper. Tell me
about your life. How did you come to be a flower-seller? What
did you do before that? Start right from the beginning.

2. You have lovely red hair, just like mine!
What's your name, child?

3. There's a good girl, Hetty. Another few spoonfuls just
for me, eh? And look what I have for you here – a little
slab of my own home-made toffee. You may suck on a
square when you've finished your porridge.

4. You are a child of Satan, Hetty Feather. You have his
Hell-red hair and his flaming temper. We must quench
this devilish fire. You must be taught a severe lesson.

5. I don't want my name in no storybook.

6. Jem says when I am quite grown up and can leave
this horrid hospital, he will come and marry me.

7. We can't go to the circus, Hetty! It's not within
close proximity! It couldn't possibly be further away.

MY TIMETABLE

Fill in your lessons here – and don't forget
your after-school clubs and practices.

TIME	MONDAY	TUESDAY
8.30		
9.00		
9.30		
10.00		
10.30		
11.00		
11.30		
12.00		
12.30		
1.00		
1.30		
2.00		
2.30		
3.00		
3.30		
4.00		
4.30		
5.00		
5.30		

MY TIMETABLE

Fill in your lessons here — and don't forget
your after-school clubs and practices.

WEDNESDAY	THURSDAY	FRIDAY

IMPORTANT BIRTHDAYS

Name: Joe

Birthday: 21st may

Name:

Birthday:

Name:

Birthday:

Name:

Birthday:

Name:

Birthday:

Name:

Birthday:

Name:

Birthday:

Name:

Birthday:

IMPORTANT BIRTHDAYS

Name:_____

Birthday:_____

Name:_____

Birthday:_____

Name:_____

Birthday:_____

Name:_____

Birthday:_____

Name:_____

Birthday:_____

Name:_____

Birthday:_____

Name:_____

Birthday:_____

Name:_____

Birthday:_____

IMPORTANT ADDRESSES

Name: _____

Address: _____

_____

Phone: _____

Email: _____

Name: _____

Address: _____

_____

Phone: _____

Email: _____

Name: _____

Address: _____

_____

Phone: _____

Email: _____

Name: _____

Address: _____

_____

Phone: _____

Email: _____

IMPORTANT ADDRESSES

Name: _____

Address: _____

_____

Phone: _____

Email: _____

Name: _____

Address: _____

_____

Phone: _____

Email: _____

Name: _____

Address: _____

_____

Phone: _____

Email: _____

Name: _____

Address: _____

_____

Phone: _____

Email: _____

JANUARY

My name is Hetty Feather. Don't mock. It's not my *real* name. I'm absolutely certain my mother would have picked a beautiful romantic name for me – though sadly I have not turned out beautiful or romantic.

January 1

January 2

January 3

January 4

January 5

January 6

January 7

January 8

January 9

January 10

January 11

January 12

January 13

January 14

January 15

January 16

January 17

January 18

January 19

January 20

January 21

January 22

January 23

January 24

January 25

January 26

January 27

January 28

January 29

January 30

January 31

Notes

THE FOUNDLING HOSPITAL

Many real children experienced childhoods similar to Hetty's, growing up in the Foundling Hospital. Thomas Coram started this 'Hospital for the Maintenance and Education of Exposed and Deserted Children' in 1739. It was the first special children's charity in the UK, and over 250 years, it rescued more than 27,000 abandoned babies and children.

The Foundling Hospital is now a museum, which you can actually visit in London, but its work is still happening today. It's now known simply as Coram, helping children who are alone or at risk, or without a real home.

You can find out more about Coram by visiting www.coram.org.uk – and you can see for yourself what life was like for children like Hetty by going to the Foundling Museum.

FEBRUARY

'You look a total sweetheart in that lovely green dress, Hetty,' Bertie said, spinning me round.

Was he saying I was his sweetheart? My heart started thumping inside my tight velvet bodice. I knew Jem assumed I was his sweetheart.

February 1

February 2

February 3

February 4

February 5

February 6

February 7

February 8

February 9

February 10

February 11

February 12

February 13

February 14

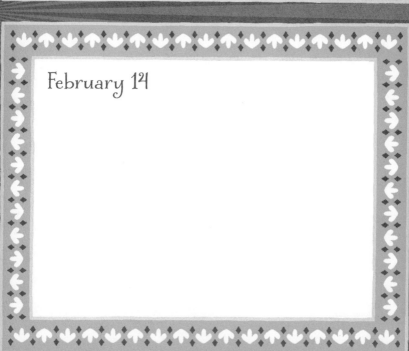

February 15

February 16

February 17

February 18

February 19

February 20

February 21

February 22

February 23

February 24

February 25

February 26

February 27

February 28

February 29

Notes

VICTORIAN VALENTINES

The tradition of sending Valentine's Day cards started
in the UK and was made popular by the Victorians.
Victorian people didn't write message or their names
on cards, though – they were always anonymous!

A very famous children's book illustrator, Kate Greenaway,
also designed Valentine's Day cards. Her designs are
now very collectable. You might have heard of the Kate
Greenaway Medal, which is awarded every year to
a different children's book illustrator.

Although Valentine's Day cards began very simply,
the Victorians started to decorate them with flower petals,
bits of lace, sachets of perfume, and even locks of hair!

One Valentine's tradition was for girls to place
green bay leaves on their pillows and sprinkle them
with rose water; they hoped they might see the face
of their true sweetheart in their dreams.

MARCH

'What on earth's that?' said Janet. 'Are they playing some kind of musical instrument?'

'Oh, Janet, I think it's the circus!' I said, running to the window. I threw back the sash and leaned out as far as I could go.

'Careful, Hetty!' she said, hanging onto me by my petticoats. 'Oh my goodness, it is a circus!'

'It's my circus!' I breathed as I peered down at a great wagon painted scarlet and emerald and canary yellow.

March 1

March 2

March 3

March 4

March 5

March 6

March 7

March 8

March 9

March 10

March 11

March 12

March 13

March 14

March 15

March 16

March 17

March 18

March 19

March 20

March 21

March 22

March 23

March 24

March 25

March 26

March 27

March 28

March 29

March 30

March 31

Notes

THE VICTORIAN CIRCUS

Hetty first encounters the circus as a little girl, and it becomes a very important part of her life. She even joins the circus and becomes its ringmaster!

The Victorians really did love the circus. Because circuses travelled to so many different cities and even small towns and villages, it was very easy for lots of people to watch their performances. Hundreds of different circuses travelled around the UK during the Victorian times.

One particularly famous circus was an American one called Barnum and Bailey's, which toured around the UK. There were at least ten displays including aquatic acts, aerialists, elephants and an equestrian act featuring 70 horses performing in the ring at once!

The most successful circus owner was named George Sanger. He was an eccentric millionaire who was known for being a smart dresser, and always wore a shiny top hat and diamond tie pin. Sanger's circus performed for Queen Victoria herself!

APRIL

'So you're a new little girl,' said the kitchen maid at the end of the table, serving out bowls of porridge.

She was small and slight – if it wasn't for her careworn face I might have mistaken her for one of the big girl foundlings. Her maid's uniform hung about her, her skirts trailing past her boots.

'I'm new here too. It feels very strange, don't it?'

I nodded forlornly.

'I'm sure we'll both settle down soon,' she said. 'Here, specially for you!' She took a twist of paper out of her apron pocket and sprinkled the contents on the top of my porridge. 'Sugar!' she whispered.

April 1

April 2

April 3

April 4

April 5

April 6

April 7

April 8

April 9

April 10

April 11

April 12

Lil

April 13

April 14

April 15

April 16

April 17

April 18

April 19

April 20

April 21

April 22

April 23

April 24

April 25

April 26

April 27

April 28

April 29

April 30

VICTORIAN FOOD AND DRINK

Rather than buying their food in supermarkets like lots of us do today, the Victorians would go to a number of separate shops to buy their goods, like the butcher's shop that Bertie works in.

There were no fridges or freezers, so fruit and vegetables couldn't be kept for very long, unless they were pickled or turned into preserves or jams. Oranges were thought of as a real treat, and often put into children's stockings on Christmas Day.

Why not try to write a menu for your own Victorian dinner party? Here are some typical Victorian foods to help you:

Mutton ★ Pork chops ★ Boiled beef ★ Pickled herrings
Porridge ★ Eggs ★ Potatoes ★ Carrots ★ Onions
Milk ★ Cheese ★ Broth ★ Bread ★ Sugar ★ Jam ★ Tea
Treacle pudding ★ Spotted dick ★ Blancmange

MAY

Dr March laid the back of his hand on my forehead, then listened to my chest. 'The child is clearly ill, Matron, wilful or not,' he said. 'She's a frail little creature and I fear her chest is weak. She must be kept here in bed, wrapped in wet sheets to lower her fever, and be fed an invalid diet of bread and milk.'

May 1

May 2

May 3

May 4

May 5

May 6

May 7

May 8

May 9

May 10

May 11

May 12

May 13

May 14

May 15

May 16

May 17

May 18

May 19

May 20

May 21

May 22

May 23

May 24

May 25

May 26

May 27

May 28

May 29

May 30

May 31

Notes

FLORENCE NIGHTINGALE

Florence Nightingale is perhaps the most famous nurse of all time, and one of the most well-known Victorians.

She looked after wounded soldiers during the Crimean War, and because she would walk around late at night to check on her patients, she became known as 'the lady with the lamp'.

Florence Nightingale started one of the first ever nursing schools in London, and thousands of nurses have taken the 'Nightingale Pledge' – a special oath said by new nurses.

JUNE

'Are you a believer, Hetty Feather?' asked Madame
Berenice. I wasn't quite sure what she meant.

'I go to church every Sunday,' I said.

'Do you believe in the psychic sciences, child?'

'I – I'm not sure what they are,' I said.

June 1

June 2

June 3

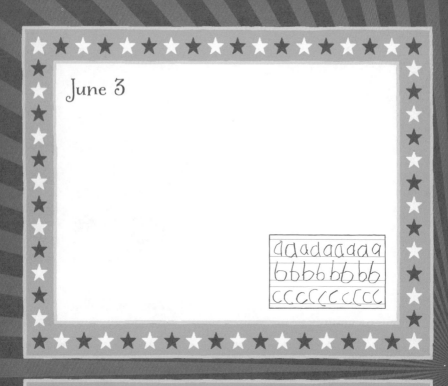

aaaaaaaaa
bbbbbbbb
ccccccccc

June 4

June 5

June 6

June 7

June 8

June 9

June 10

June 11

June 12

June 13

June 14

June 15

June 16

June 17

June 18

June 19

June 20

June 21

June 22

June 23

June 24

June 25

June 26

June 27

June 28

June 29

June 30

VICTORIAN SPIRITUALISTS

Spiritualists believe that the spirits of people who have died can communicate with the living. This belief was very popular with the Victorians, and people like Hetty's fellow servant Sarah would happily pay money to someone like Madame Berenice, who claimed to be able to hear the spirits and would pass on messages.

Lots of the most famous Spiritualists became very rich by conducting séances, like the one Hetty and Sarah attend – although some of them did admit later on that everything they had claimed was just a trick!

JULY

'I have a very important announcement to make, children,' Matron Bottomly said. 'As you all know, our dear Queen has ruled over us for fifty wonderful years. Next Thursday is the day of the Golden Jubilee, when the whole country will celebrate her glorious reign. We are going to celebrate too! You have all been invited to a festive gathering at Hyde Park in London. You will be given a splendid meal at this venue and join in all kinds of fun and games, and then Her Majesty the Queen herself will come and greet you!'

July 1

July 2

July 3

July 4

July 5

July 6

July 7

July 8

July 9

July 10

July 11

July 12

July 13

July 14

July 15

July 16

July 17

July 18

July 19

July 20

July 21

July 22

July 23

July 24

July 25

July 26

July 27

July 28

July 29

July 30

July 31

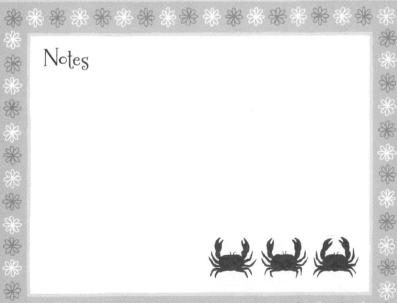

Notes

QUEEN VICTORIA'S GOLDEN JUBILEE

Queen Victoria celebrated fifty years on the throne with huge celebrations.

On 20th June 1887 she held a banquet at Buckingham Palace, where fifty foreign kings and princes were invited. Queen Victoria wrote this in her diary:

Had a large family dinner. All the Royalties assembled in the Bow Room, and we dined in the Supper-room, which looked splendid with the buffet covered with the gold plate. The table was a large horseshoe one, with many lights on it. The King of Denmark took me in, and Willy of Greece sat on my other side. The Princes were all in uniform, and the Princesses were all beautifully dressed. Afterwards we went into the Ballroom, where my band played.

On the following day she took part in a procession through London, in a carriage pulled by six cream-coloured horses. A celebration for 27,000 children took place in Hyde Park, which is where Hetty and her fellow foundlings would have been taken! Every child who attended was given a special mug as a souvenir.

AUGUST

Charlotte and Maisie raced round a corner. I heard them whooping triumphantly. I followed them, and then stopped short, my heart thudding. I'd seen pictures of the sea in books, each wave carefully cross-hatched to give a life-like impression. I'd seen the Thames, which had seemed vast enough after the country stream of my childhood. But nothing had prepared me for the immensity of this sea glittering before me in the sunlight.

August 1

August 2

August 3

August 4

August 5

August 6

August 7

August 8

August 9

August 10

August 11

August 12

August 13

August 14

August 15

August 16

August 17

August 18

August 19

August 20

August 21

August 22

August 23

August 24

August 25

August 26

August 27

August 28

August 29

August 30

August 31

Notes

THE VICTORIAN SEASIDE

During Queen Victoria's reign, travelling by train became much more easy and affordable, so families who had enough money took day trips to the seaside – or even a longer holiday, like the lovely Greenwood family who befriend Hetty.

Some of the most popular seaside towns were Blackpool, Southend and Brighton. People enjoyed doing lots of the same things we do on seaside holidays today: eating fish and chips and ice creams (also known as hokey pokeys), making sandcastles, paddling in the sea (although not many people could actually swim) and riding on donkeys. Punch and Judy shows and music hall performances were also very popular.

You would never have seen Victorian people dressed in the swimming trunks and bikinis we wear today! Instead, they wore bathing costumes that covered up most of their bodies, and they'd get changed into them in special wooden huts called bathing machines.

SEPTEMBER

I worked very hard on her nightgown. I knew Mother would have been perfectly content with a plain gown, straight up and down, with no frills or furbelows. She wouldn't even have minded if the stitching was big so long as the seams held fast. But I sewed fancy stitches all the same, and finished the gown with three ruffles instead of an ordinary hem, and I embroidered an entire flower garden on the yoke: red roses, yellow daffodils, purple pansies and blue cornflowers, with a little green trail of ivy twining round all of them.

September 1

September 2

September 3

September 4

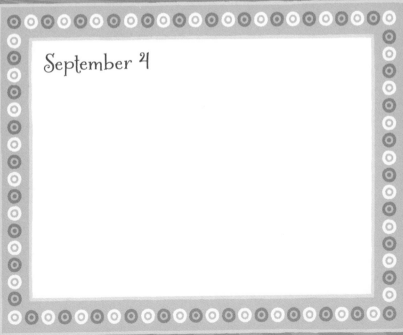

September 5

September 6

September 7

September 8

September 9

September 10

September 11

September 12

September 13

September 14

September 15

September 16

September 17

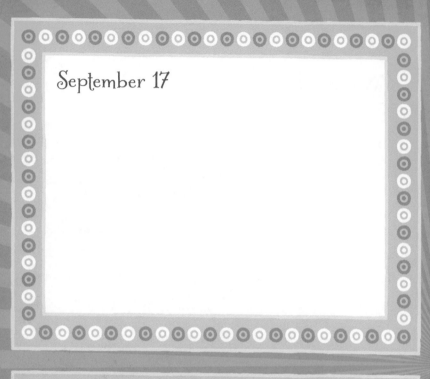

September 18

September 19

September 20

September 21

September 22

September 23

September 24

September 25

September 26

September 27

September 28

September 29

September 30

VICTORIAN FASHION

Do you think you would have enjoyed dressing up
in the elaborate gowns of a well-to-do Victorian lady like
Miss Sarah Smith? They look lots of fun to wear, but
Victorian fashion was very uncomfortable!

Corsets were worn by ladies underneath their dresses to
give them a tiny waist. It often took two people – perhaps
maids or sisters – to squeeze a lady into her corset, and
women sometimes fainted because they weren't able to
breathe properly. It would have been difficult to eat
while wearing a corset – as Hetty discovers when she
tackles an enormous Christmas dinner!

The Victorians loved decoration, so dresses were made
of rich materials with ruffles, collars and fancy buttons.
Gloves were always worn, and ladies tried to keep their
hands as pale and soft as possible, as that was a sign
of beauty. Enormous hats with ribbons, flowers
and long feathers were also very popular!

OCTOBER

'Sapphire is so elegant, so romantic. It's a perfect name for a writer,' I said, signing it in the air with a flourish.

'Let us hope you become one, then,' said Mama, a little tartly.

'You wait and see. I will publish my memoirs and make our fortune. Miss Smith will help me. My story will be turned into a proper book with gold lettering and a fancy picture on the front.'

October 1

October 2

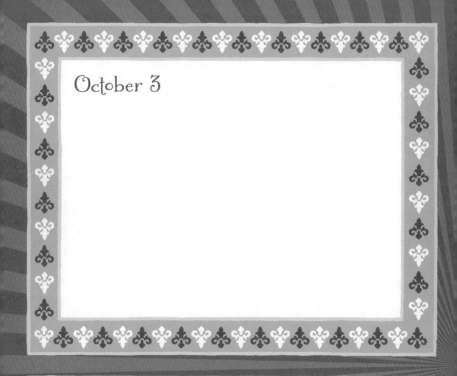

October 3

October 4

October 5

October 6

October 7

October 8

October 9

October 10

October 11

October 12

October 13

October 14

October 15

October 16

October 17

October 18

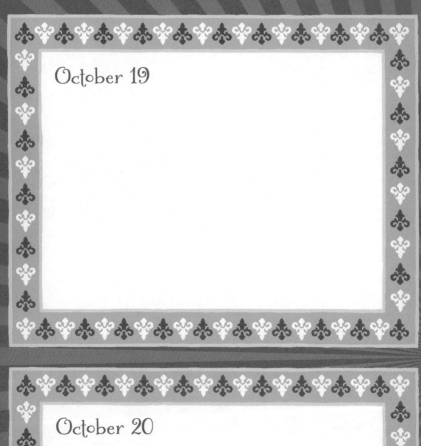

October 19

October 20

October 21

October 22

October 23

October 24

October 25

October 26

October 27

October 28

October 29

October 30

October 31

Notes

VICTORIAN WRITERS

Lots of the most famous writers of all time were Victorians!

Charles Dickens is probably the best-known Victorian writer. His books include *Great Expectations*, *A Tale of Two Cities* – which is thought to be the best-selling novel of all time – and *A Christmas Carol*.

Lewis Carroll was a mathematician before he was a writer. One day he took a boat trip along the river in Oxford with some family friends, including ten-year old Alice Pleasance Liddell. Alice asked him to tell her a story, which became *Alice's Adventures in Wonderland*.

Frances Hodgson Burnett wrote three classic children's books: *The Secret Garden*, *Little Lord Fauntleroy*, and *A Little Princess*. She was English, but lived for years in America. She returned to England for Queen Victoria's Golden Jubilee – so she may have walked right past Hetty Feather!

Sir Arthur Conan Doyle created the famous detective Sherlock Holmes. Nearly 100 years after Conan Doyle's death, thousands of people still visit Baker Street in London – where Sherlock Holmes lived – every year.

NOVEMBER

I sat flicking through my memoir books, wondering
if there were any point in taking them too. I decided
I couldn't relinquish them. I wrote Hetty Feather
on the first, Sapphire Battersea on the second,
and Emerald Star on the third. I packed them
away carefully, wondering if they might ever be
properly published.

November 1

November 2

November 3

November 4

November 5

November 6

November 7

November 8

November 9

November 10

November 11

November 12

November 13

November 14

November 15

November 16

November 17

November 18

November 19

November 20

November 21

November 22

November 23

November 24

November 25

November 26

November 27

November 28

November 29

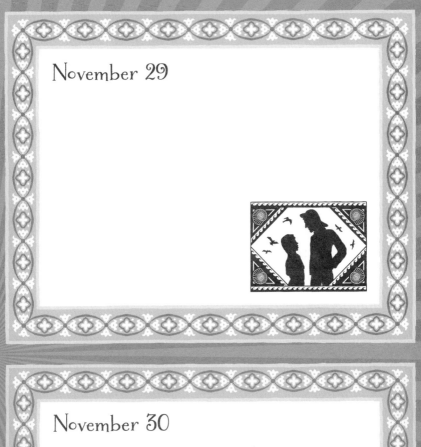

November 30

HETTY'S GLITTERING GEMSTONES

Hetty learns that her real mother named her Sapphire, which is a precious blue gemstone. She also gives herself a new name for when she performs: Emerald – another precious stone, but this one is green! Can you match all the stones below to their colours and descriptions?

RUBY DIAMOND AQUAMARINE
JADE JET PEARL AMBER

A. Often used to make pretty necklaces, these stones are created inside mollusks such as oysters and mussels.

B. One of the world's strongest materials. These stones are often used in sparkling engagement rings, and have had songs written about them!

C. A green stone which was very popular in China and used to create beautiful carvings.

D. A warm orange-gold stone made from fossilized tree resin.

E. A black stone which is often polished to a shine and used to make jewellery. Lots of this stone is found in Whitby in Yorkshire – perhaps near to where Hetty's parents came from!

F. A blood-red stone which is the birthstone for July.

G. A light blue or green stone, the birthstone for March.

DECEMBER

We ate turkey, the very first time I'd tasted it. We had roast potatoes too, crisp and golden, and parsnips and carrots and small green sprouts like baby cabbages. We ate until we were nearly bursting, but when we were offered a second serving we said yes please, and Mother nodded enthusiastically. There were puddings too – a rich figgy pudding with a custard, a pink blancmange like a fairy castle, and a treacle tart with whipped cream. I could not choose which pudding I wanted because they all looked so wonderful, so I had a portion of each.

December 1

December 2

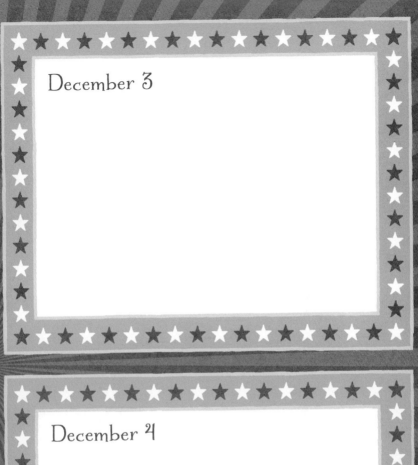

December 3

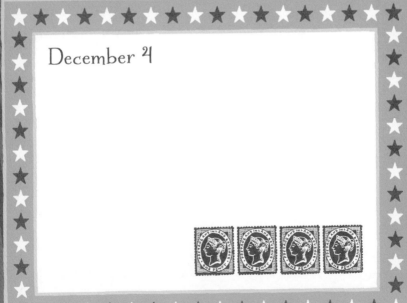

December 4

December 5

December 6

December 7

December 8

December 9

December 10

December 11

December 12

December 13

December 14

December 15

December 16

December 17

December 18

December 19

December 20

December 21

December 22

December 23

December 24

December 25

December 26

December 27

December 28

December 29

December 30

December 31

Notes

HETTY'S VICTORIAN
🌿 CHRISTMAS 🌿

Lots of the Christmas traditions we have today come
from the Victorian times, when Hetty would have
celebrated Christmas.

Before Queen Victoria was on the throne, most people didn't
have a Christmas tree. When she married Prince Albert,
who was from Germany, he introduced her to the German
tradition of decorating a tree. A newspaper published a
drawing of the royal family with their tree, and many
families decided to copy the idea. Soon every home had
its own tree covered in fruit, sweets, gifts and candles.

The first Christmas cards were invented by Henry Cole in
1843. He asked his friend John Horsley, an artist, to draw
the picture for the front of the card: a family enjoying
Christmas dinner together, and people helping the poor.
Within a few years, the tradition of sending a card
at Christmas had taken off.

The Christmas cracker is a Victorian invention, too!
Tom Smith, a sweetmaker, noticed packages of sugared
almonds wrapped in twists of paper when he visited Paris
in 1848. They gave him the idea of the cracker: packages
of sweets that would burst apart when pulled! Later, the
sweets were replaced with paper hats, jokes and gifts.

ANSWERS

HETTY FEATHER QUIZ:

1. 25621.
2. Peg
3. An elephant
4. Flowers.
5. An under-housemaid.
6. To become a soldier.
7. Her mother.
8. A mermaid

9. Mina and Ezra.
10. A waistcoat and pocket watch.
11. Janet
12. Ringmaster.
13. The Silver Boys.
14. Lucy.
15. A monkey.

WHO SAID IT?

1. Miss Sarah Smith
2. Madame Adeline
3. Ida
4. Matron Bottomly
5. Sissy
6. Eliza
7. Gideon

GEMSTONES:

Ruby – F
Diamond – B
Aquamarine – G
Jade – C
Jet – E
Pearl – A
Amber – D

Have you read all the *Hetty Feather* adventures?

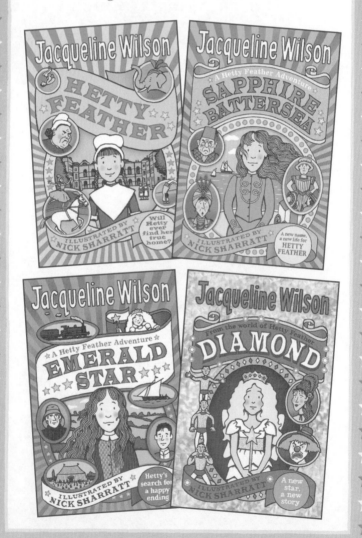

Have you seen this other
gorgeous stationery?

Dream Journal

Jacqueline Wilson

Hobby Journal

Jacqueline Wilson
ILLUSTRATED BY NICK SHARRATT

HAVE YOU READ THEM ALL?

WHERE TO START

THE DINOSAUR'S PACKED LUNCH
THE MONSTER STORY-TELLER

FOR YOUNGER READERS

BURIED ALIVE! ✓
CLIFFHANGER
GLUBBSLYME
LIZZIE ZIPMOUTH
SLEEPOVERS
THE CAT MUMMY
THE MUM-MINDER
THE WORRY WEBSITE

FIRST CLASS FRIENDS

BAD GIRLS
BEST FRIENDS
SECRETS
VICKY ANGEL

HISTORICAL ADVENTURES

OPAL PLUMSTEAD ✓
QUEENIE
THE LOTTIE PROJECT

ALL ABOUT JACQUELINE WILSON

JACKY DAYDREAM
MY SECRET DIARY

FAMILY DRAMAS

CANDYFLOSS
CLEAN BREAK
COOKIE
FOUR CHILDREN AND IT ✓
LILY ALONE ✓
LITTLE DARLINGS
LOLA ROSE
MIDNIGHT
THE BED AND BREAKFAST STAR
THE ILLUSTRATED MUM
THE LONGEST WHALE SONG
THE SUITCASE KID
KATY

FOR OLDER READERS

DUSTBIN BABY
GIRLS IN LOVE
GIRLS IN TEARS
GIRLS OUT LATE
GIRLS UNDER PRESSURE
KISS
LOVE LESSONS
MY SISTER JODIE

MOST POPULAR CHARACTERS

HETTY FEATHER ✓
SAPPHIRE BATTERSEA ✓
EMERALD STAR ✓
DIAMOND
THE STORY OF TRACY BEAKER
THE DARE GAME
STARRING TRACY BEAKER ✓

STORIES ABOUT SISTERS

DOUBLE ACT ✓
THE BUTTERFLY CLUB ✓
THE DIAMOND GIRLS
THE WORST THING
ABOUT MY SISTER ✓

ALSO AVAILABLE

PAWS AND WHISKERS
THE JACQUELINE WILSON
CHRISTMAS CRACKER
THE JACQUELINE WILSON TREASURY

THE HETTY FEATHER JOURNAL
A DOUBLEDAY BOOK 978 0 857 53450 7

First published in Great Britain by Doubleday,
an imprint of Random House Children's Publishers UK
A Penguin Random House Company

Penguin
Random House
UK

This edition published 2015

1 3 5 7 9 10 8 6 4 2

FSC
www.fsc.org
MIX
Paper from
responsible sources
FSC® C018179

Set in Liam

RANDOM HOUSE CHILDREN'S PUBLISHERS UK
61–63 Uxbridge Road, London W5 5SA

www.randomhousechildrens.co.uk
www.totallyrandombooks.co.uk
www.randomhouse.co.uk

Addresses for companies within The Random House Group Limited
can be found at: www.randomhouse.co.uk/offices.htm

THE RANDOM HOUSE GROUP Limited Reg. No. 954009

A CIP catalogue record for this book is available from the British Library.

Printed and bound in China